Mischief

by Karen Anderson

illustrated by Nic Marshall

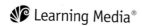 Learning Media®

Contents

1. Plans for the Summer

email

From: Tyler

Ranch

Hi Tania

Let's go to the ranch again this summer. I'm sure Grandma and Grandpa would *love* to see us! Email me.

From Tyler

From: Tania

Ranch and rodeo

Hi Tyler

Sure thing! I'll ask Grandma and Grandpa. I'll ask if we can go when the county rodeo is on.

I've got a plan!

From Tania

May 10

Dear Grandma and Grandpa,

Can I come stay on the ranch again this summer? Can Tyler come, too? We had a great time last summer. I think Grandpa's bull must be missing us. We spent so much time together.

From,

Tania

P.S. I hope you like the picture I drew for you.

P.P.S. When is the county rodeo?

Tyler and me
patting the bull.
by Tania

May 17

Dear Tania,

We do remember the last time you and your cousin Tyler stayed on the ranch.

We had planned to go to Florida for the summer, but I guess we can go when you're in school.

Why do you want to know when the rodeo is?

See you in July.

Love from,

Grandma and Grandpa

2. Clown Costume

From: Tania

Ranch and rodeo and clown

Hi Tyler

Grandma and Grandpa said yes! We can go the first week in July. I think they've forgotten about the time we used Grandma's makeup to put on your clown face for the rodeo. They might be suspicious about the rodeo plan, though.

Can I be the clown this time?

I can't wait for summer! Only 42 days to go.

Love from Tania

From: Tyler

Rodeo clown

Hi Tania

I think you should be the rodeo clown because you can run the fastest.

40 days to go!

Love from Tyler

From: Tania

Whale music and belts

Hi Tyler

Mom said Grandpa will probably be exhausted by the time we leave the ranch. She said he should listen to whale music to calm him down.

Bring as many of your Dad's belts as you can. We'll need them to hold onto the bull.

Only 36 days to go.

Your buddy, Tania

13

From: Tyler

Belts and ugly pants

Hi Tania

I'll bring Dad's belts and the bright orange tie he wore when he was dating Mom. Yuk! But they're great for a clown.

Can you bring your mom's ugly pants (the baggy, flowery ones)? And her red shoes?

I think we're in for an exciting vacation this year – we might even ride the bull!

35 days.

Your best buddy, Tyler

3. Bullying the Bull

From: Tania

Ugly pants and whale music

Hi Tyler

I've packed Mom's pants and shoes already. I've also packed one of her whale music CDs. I thought we could use it to calm the bull. I hope Grandma and Grandpa have a CD player that we can sneak outside.

32 days!

Your best buddy ever, Tania

From: Tyler

Whale music and grandparents

Howdy Tania

For our own safety, I think we need to make the bull as calm as possible before ... you know what!

We may need to play the whale music to Grandma and Grandpa too if they find out what our plan is!

One month to go!

Your partner in adventures,
Tyler

From: Tania

Hammer and nails

Howdy Tyler

Can you bring a hammer and nails? We need to build a chute to catch the bull so we can ride him. Here's a picture of my idea.

28 days.

Your partner in amazing adventures, Tania

Chute
Plan

4. Change of Plans

email

From: Tyler

That's a great chute

Howdy Tania

Thanks for the picture.

Only 23 more days.

Your partner in extra-amazing adventures, Tyler

From: Tania

Clown and cowboy

Howdy Tyler

If I have to dress up like a clown, I think you should dress up like a cowboy. Do you still have your cowboy hat and chaps?

See you in 19 days.

Your partner in super-extra-amazing adventures, Tania

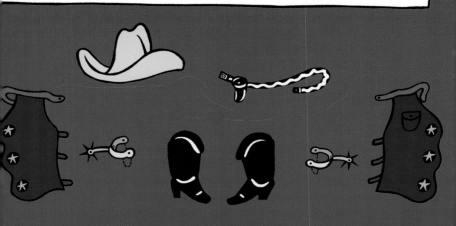

email

From: Tyler

Cowboy and school

Howdy Tania

OK, then. I'll be a cowboy.

Just 11 days to go – and it's the last week of school!

Your partner for ever and ever, Tyler

From: Tania

Being nice

Howdy Tyler

I'm all packed and ready to go. I wonder if we can get Grandpa to drive us to the rodeo?

I think we should both write Grandma and Grandpa. It'll help to put them in a good mood before we arrive. But BE CAREFUL! Don't give away our plan!

Only 9 more days.

Your partner for ever and ever and ever, Tania

June 22

Dear Grandma and Grandpa,

I love you, Grandma. I love you, Grandpa. Here's a picture of Mom and me.

Love from,

Tania

June 23

Dear Grandma and Grandpa,

Thanks for letting Tania and me come stay. We're looking forward to helping you out on the ranch.

Love from,

Tyler

P.S. Grandpa, can you drive us to the county rodeo?

June 25

Dear Sir/Madam,

   We would like to buy tickets for two children and two adults to fly to Florida next week. If you don't have any tickets for Florida, anywhere else in the world will do.

   Yours sincerely,

   Desperate grandparents

June 25

Dear Tyler,

Thank you for your letter. You didn't tell us you wanted to go to the county rodeo – again!

We've decided to go to Florida after all. But we'll take you and Tania with us. We're sure we'll all have a great time together.

Love from,

Grandma and Grandpa

Fly with Us
123 The Avenue • Local Town • Texas

June 27

Dear Mr. and Mrs. Rancher,

Here are your tickets to Florida.

We have also sent you four free tickets to the Florida Rodeo Fun Park.

We do hope that you enjoy your vacation.

Yours sincerely,

F. Day
Travel Agent